Welcome to The Giggle Club

The Giggle Club is a collection of new picture books made to put a giggle into early reading. There are funny stories about a contrary mouse, a dancing fox, a turtle with a trumpet, a pig with a ball, a hungry monster, a laughing lobster, an elephant who sneezes away the jungle and lots more! Each of these characters is a member of **The Giggle Club**, but anyone can join: just pick up a **Giggle Club** book, read it and get giggling!

Turn to the checklist on the inside back cover and tick off the Giggle Club books you have read.

TEE HEE!

HA HA!

For Carol
P. R.

For little Sophie,
my great-niece,
with love
H.C.

First published 1996 by Walker Books Ltd
87 Vauxhall Walk, London SE11 5HJ

This edition published 1997

Text © 1996 Phyllis Root
Illustrations © 1996 Helen Craig

4 6 8 10 9 7 5 3

Printed in Hong Kong

This book has been typeset in Calligraphic Antique.

British Library Cataloguing in Publication Data
A catalogue record for this book is available
from the British Library.

ISBN 0-7445-5461-6

ONE WINDY WEDNESDAY

Written by
PHYLLIS ROOT

Illustrated by
HELEN CRAIG

WALKER BOOKS
AND SUBSIDIARIES
LONDON · BOSTON · SYDNEY

One Wednesday, Bonnie Bumble felt the wind begin to blow.

It blew the
quack right out
of the duck.

QUACK!

It blew the moo
right out of
the cow.

MOO!

It blew the
oink right out
of the pig.

It blew the baa
right out of
the lamb.

"Moo!" said the duck.

When the wind died down
she worked to put everything right.

QUACK!

She patted the
quack back on
to the duck.

She hitched
the moo back
on to the cow.

MOO!

She tied the oink back
on to the pig.

She knitted the baa
back on to the lamb.

"Oink!"
said the pig.

"That's better," said
Bonnie Bumble,
all worn out.

"Baa!"
said the lamb.

Just then a little breeze blew by.
"Meow, meow, meow,"
said the dog!